SNOWBOUND

SNOWBOUND

The Tragic Story of the Donner Party

by DAVID LAVENDER

Holiday House / New York

To the children of the Donner Party—those whose lives were lost and those who lived with the memories.

Library of Congress Cataloging-in-Publication Data
Lavender, David Sievert, 1910–
Snowbound : the tragic story of the Donner Party / David Lavender.
p.   cm.
Includes bibliographical references and index.
Summary: Relates the ordeals faced by a group of pioneers on their
journey from Illinois to California in 1846.
ISBN 0-8234-1231-8
1. Donner Party—Juvenile literature.   [1. Donner Party.]
I. Title.

F868.N5L38   1996   95-41266   CIP   AC
978—dc20

Contents

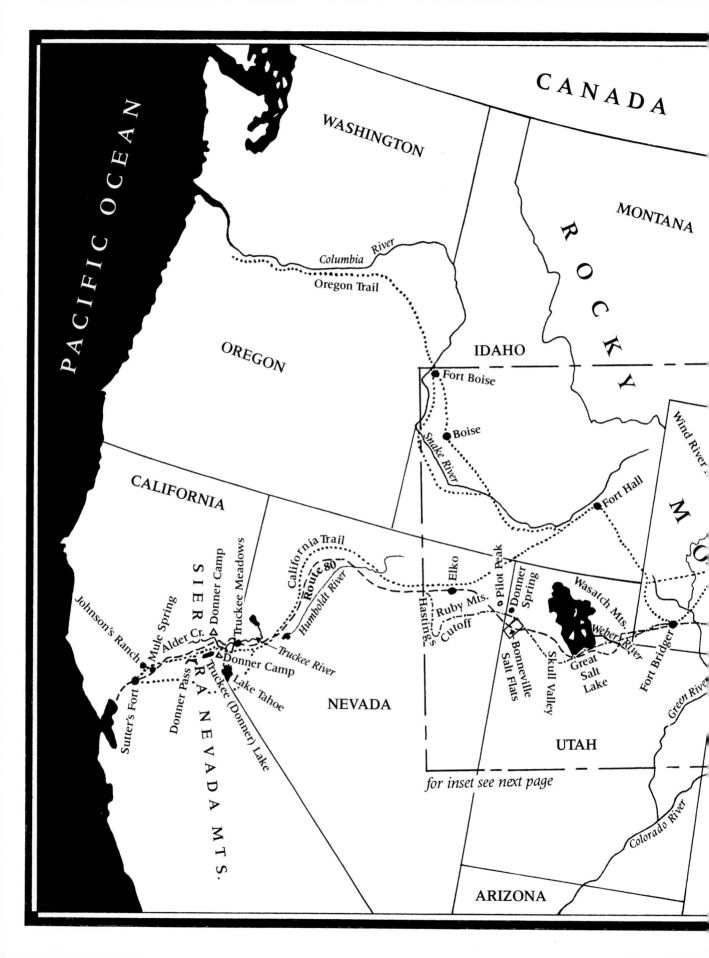

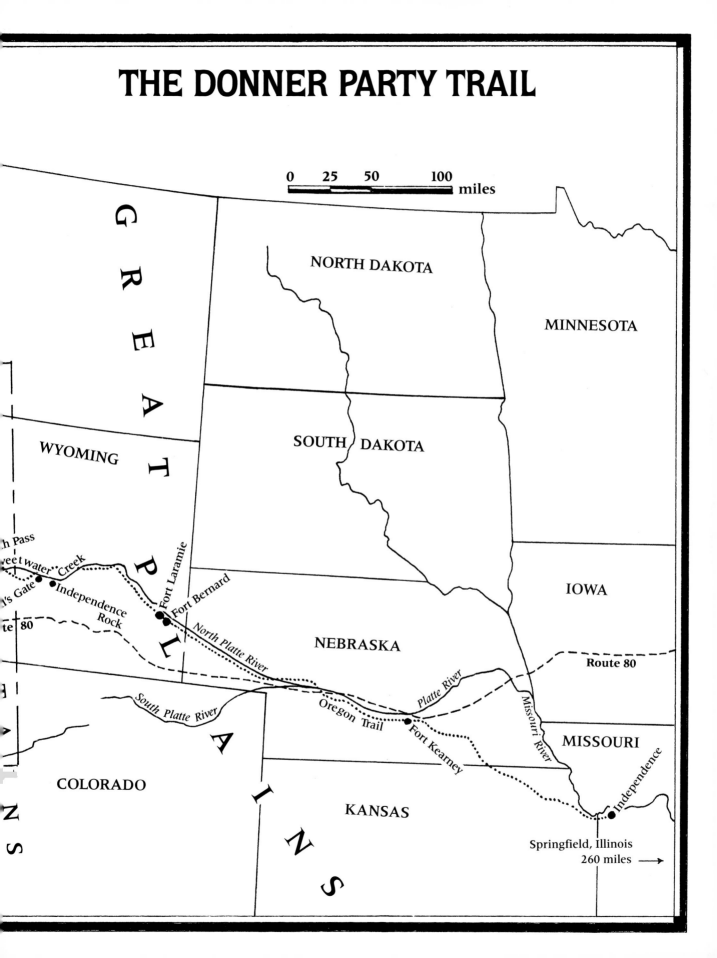

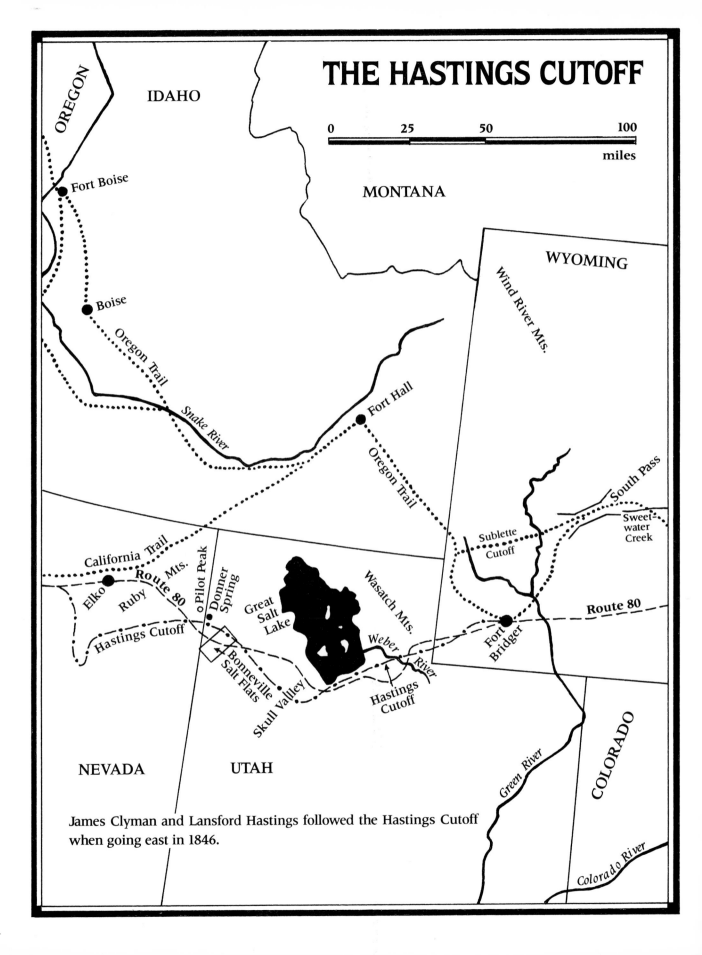

THE HASTINGS CUTOFF

James Clyman and Lansford Hastings followed the Hastings Cutoff when going east in 1846.

I

Looking West

Several times during the icy winter of 1845–1846, the brothers Jacob and George Donner and their friend James Frazier Reed met to discuss selling nearly everything they owned. They would then be free to move with their families from Springfield, Illinois, to California.

Most of their neighbors thought the three men had lost their senses. California! It was two thousand, perhaps twenty-five hundred miles away. Sure, parties of emigrants had been going to Oregon for the past ten years or so, their wagon trains guided by fur trappers who knew the best trails through the rugged western land. But going to California was different. The few people who went there had to leave the Oregon route somewhere beyond the Rocky Mountains and travel on west through barren areas no one knew much about. There were rumors of skyscraping mountains, terrible deserts, and hostile Indians.

California itself, the neighbors went on, belonged to Mexico, and the Mexican government was quarreling angrily with the United States about the ownership of Texas. Suppose war broke out and the Mexican authorities

in California expelled or imprisoned all Americans inside the province's boundary. What would the Donners do then?

Age was another handicap. Jacob Donner was sixty-five. His brother George was sixty-two. Although James Reed was only forty-six, he planned to take his mother-in-law along. She was seventy and in ill health. Nevertheless, she was determined to go. Such elderly people were bound to suffer on the long trail.

The wives of the Donners and James Reed were considerably younger than their husbands. Jacob's wife, Elizabeth, and George's wife, Tamsen, a former schoolteacher, were both forty-five. Reed's wife, Margaret, was thirty-two. All three men had been married more than once, so that some of the children in each family had been born to different mothers. There were sixteen children altogether. Their ages ranged from two to fourteen. Surely, the neighbors said, it was irresponsible for so few adults to take so many children into a wilderness.

Why were the families doing it? That question baffled the neighbors. The Donners and Jim Reed had no need to ride west in search of opportunities. The brothers were prosperous farmers. Reed was getting on well as a maker of furniture. Springfield, on whose outskirts they lived, was an established city. Since 1840 it had been the capital of Illinois. Why did respected citizens want to trade security like that for an unguessable future in a strange land?

The Donners and Jim Reed refused to listen. They had placed their faith in a book entitled *The Emigrants' Guide to Oregon and California*. Its author, Lansford W. Hastings, had gone to Oregon with a small wagon train in 1842. The next

The town square of Springfield, capital city of Illinois, looked like this when Jacob and George Donner decided to journey to California, in wagons, with their families in 1846. Illinois State Historical Society

The Donners, Reeds, and many others were lured west, in part, by an undependable guidebook written by Lansford W. Hastings. UTAH STATE HISTORICAL SOCIETY

year he had ridden south from Oregon to California. After looking around for a while he had returned through Mexico to the United States. He knew what he was talking about, or so it seemed, when he published his *Guide* in Cincinnati, Ohio, early in 1845. According to the newspapers, he had started back from Ohio to California in August of that same year. With him went a party of confident emigrants. Since their departure, no further information about them had filtered back to Springfield.

The Donners and Reed understood the urge to move. They had felt in their own blood the hope for gain, and the sense of adventure that was pushing the American frontier steadily westward. George Donner, for example, had traveled from North Carolina to Kentucky, Indiana, and Illinois before going to Texas and then coming back to Springfield. All of them knew how to handle wagons. All were at ease with horses and cattle. In fact, thirteen-year-old Virginia Reed had a hot-blooded horse of her own that she rode with reckless abandon.

Most important, Hastings' words had brought a golden glow to the name California. December there was like May in the eastern United States, he said. Livestock did not have to be kept in dirty, frigid barns while blizzards raged outside. The California soil was amazingly fertile. Crops flourished during days of almost constant sunshine. The malarial fevers and congestive lungs (probably pneumonia) that were common throughout the Mississippi Valley were unknown in California. There, Hastings said, everyone was healthy. Everyone lived to a happy old age.

The Donners read those descriptions over and over. They had worked hard during their lives and found the bitter winters of Illinois increasingly hard to bear. If they went to California, they told each other, they would finish out their lives in an almost magical climate. And if they were among the early settlers there, they could buy choice land at cheap prices—land on which their children could establish fine farms and huge cattle ranches.

They wouldn't be going alone into danger, they told their neighbors. Each of them would take teamsters along to help with the wagons, and herders to drive the extra oxen, horses, and milk cows they would take west with them. Moreover, they would meet, in Independence, Missouri, other emigrants attracted to California by Hastings' *Guide*. By joining with them, they could form a wagon train strong enough to overcome whatever hazards they met along the way.

✷The *Guide* even told what kind of rough clothes to wear and how much food to take. Each grown-up would need two hundred pounds of flour, some cornmeal and hardtack, and a large basket of dried fruit. They'd want a supply of fat bacon. It would keep well if it was carried along buried in bran. They'd need some jerky, salt, sugar, tea, and coffee. Pickles brought freshness back to dry mouths. And once the train reached the Great Plains, they would be able to hunt antelope and buffalo for meat. Of course they would have to take along guns and powder and lead for hunting, as well as for protection in case of an Indian attack.✷

Another thing that struck the Donners' attention was Hastings' remark in the *Guide* about a new trail to California. In the past the few emigrants who wanted to reach California by land had started out along the well-marked Oregon Trail. After crossing the Continental Divide, that road turned northwest to a rest stop at Fort Hall in what is now southeastern Idaho. Near Fort Hall, emigrants bound for California left the Oregon Trail. They slanted southwest for scores of miles to what became known as the Humboldt River. They then followed the Humboldt almost to the foothills of the Sierra Nevada Mountains of California.

Northwest, then southwest. Surely California travelers could shorten the distance by going directly west. In his guidebook, Hastings implied that he had recently discovered such a shortcut. After crossing the Continental Divide, Californians should turn southwest, not northwest. They should skirt the southern end of a vast inland sea called Great Salt Lake. They should then head almost due west until they reached the Humboldt River.

Almost surely the Donner brothers and James Reed

The white signpost above marks a segment of the Hastings Cutoff. The road led through grim deserts stretching from western Utah into eastern Nevada, states that in 1846 had not yet been formed. STEPHEN TRIMBLE, PHOTOGRAPHER

recognized the vagueness in the book's description of the new trail. But they did not question it. They wanted to believe Hastings, because his shortcut would save time and distance. Such savings could be very important to people traveling thousands of miles with wagons.

What the Donners didn't know was this. When Hastings wrote his description, he had never seen the proposed shortcut. He was following his own secret plan. During his brief visit to California in 1845, he had acquired a large grant of land in the Sacramento Valley. His idea was to divide that land into smaller pieces he could sell at a profit to newcomers from the United States. He also wanted to build a town on his land.

He had included Oregon in his guidebook because most of the emigrants of the early 1840s preferred going to the Northwest. They would buy his book on seeing the name "Oregon" in its title. As they read, they would notice that most of the space was given to California. A paradise! The author scarcely mentioned Mexico, as though settlers needn't worry about that nation. Anything to bring people to his land!

The Donners played right into his hands when they decided, even before they left Springfield, to follow his suggestions.

II

On the Move

The Donner Party, attended by half a dozen family dogs, reached Independence, Missouri, during the first week of May 1846. They found the town's muddy, rain-swept streets jammed with American frontiersmen dressed in buckskin, Indians in blankets, and Mexicans wearing high-peaked hats called sombreros. Stores were crowded with emigrants in heavy boots and work-soiled trousers of brown homespun. The shoppers wanted an almost endless variety of items—flour and frying pans, tin cups, shovels, saws, hammers, axes, lengths of rope and chain, spare wagon spokes and oxbows, even bottles of vile-looking medicine.

This jostling mob was the tag end of a record-breaking number of westbound emigrants. During that spring, about twelve hundred men, women, and children—even nursing babies—started for Oregon. They had three hundred wagons and several thousand head of livestock. During that same spring, roughly eight hundred people, two hundred wagons, and large herds of oxen (including those that pulled the wagons), saddle horses, milk cows, and beef cattle headed toward California. Nobody knew what route to the Mexican province was best.

As the Donners sloshed across the rain-wet meadows surrounding the town, they studied the outfits of the other travelers. They must have decided theirs was as good as any. Each of the three families had three lightweight but sturdy wagons. With one exception, the vehicles were of the kind called farm wagons. Each bed was ten feet long and four feet wide, and was rimmed with sideboards two feet high. Their white tops were made of two layers of canvas waterproofed with linseed oil. Each canvas rested

The Donner group and most of the other emigrants bound for the Pacific coast traveled in ordinary farm wagons. Most also took their family dogs along. NATIONAL PARK SERVICE, JACK UNRUH, ARTIST

on five upright bows made of pliant hickory wood. There were five feet or so of space between the top of the canvas arch and the wagon's wooden bed. This space was for equipment or food. The travelers would have to shelter themselves at night under the wagons or in tents.

The one exception to this pattern was the oversized wagon James Reed built for his wife Margaret and her mother, Sarah Keyes. Neither woman was suited for the adventure. Margaret suffered from frequent headaches, but they hoped she would be better in California. Sarah, as mentioned, was seventy years old. To make traveling easier for the two women, Reed had constructed a wagon that was a mobile home. It had two floors. One was about a foot and a half above the other. The space between the floors was divided into compartments for holding food, bedding, dishes, books, and so on. The room's canvas top arched more than a foot higher than the tops of the other wagons. The inside of the wagon held two comfortable seats, two bunks, and a sheet-iron stove. Margaret Reed's two youngest children, a boy five and another three, could share the room with their mother and grandmother, particularly during stormy nights. Other women in the train could drop by to knit, chat, and have tea. Very nice—but many emigrants regarded the top-heavy wagon doubtfully. Would it hold together during the long, rough journey to California?

Like most of the emigrants, the Donner group had chosen to use oxen rather than mules for pulling their nine wagons. Oxen were stronger than mules and were much cheaper to buy. The men figured that three yokes (six oxen) could pull a single wagon loaded with fifteen hundred pounds over a long distance without becoming worn

The Donners, Reeds, and others who had come from Springfield with them joined a big wagon train a few miles out of Independence, Missouri. They traveled stretched out single file. The heavily loaded Donner wagons used three yokes (six animals) for each wagon.

out. The Reeds' big wagon, however, would need eight oxen (four yokes).

Generally speaking, a teamster stayed with the same oxen and wagon throughout a trip. It was hard work. At the end of a day's travel, the wagons were parked in a circle that had one opening in it. The oxen were unyoked inside the circle and then let out to graze during the night. At dawn the night herders drove the work animals back inside the circle. There each teamster caught the animals he was responsible for. He then yoked them to the wagon they were accustomed to pulling.

The yoke was a heavy wooden beam that held each pair of oxen side by side. It was placed on top of the animals' necks, just behind their horns. It was kept from sliding around by two U-shaped wooden oxbows. These bows were fitted under the animals' necks, with the U section underneath. The upper ends slid into holes drilled through the yoke.

Most teamsters were young men who wanted to go west but lacked money enough to put an outfit together. So they took jobs helping people who already had the proper equipment. Their pay was food for the long journey, a little clothing, and space in one of the wagons for a sack or two containing their personal possessions. In rain or snow, in

As night falls, the migrants park their wagons in a circle. SCOTT'S BLUFF NATIONAL MONUMENT, WILLIAM HENRY JACKSON, ARTIST

dust and heat they walked beside their animals, shouting commands. "Giddup!" meant start. "Gee!" was the signal to turn right and "Haw!" to turn left. "Whoa!" meant stop.

The wagons were so heavily loaded there wasn't room enough for many people to ride. Besides, the vehicles had no springs, and the journey over the roadless land was uncomfortable. So most of the people walked, except for those who were too old or were sick or were women with babies.

Wagon owners often acted as their own teamsters. But Jacob and George Donner decided to ride horseback beside their wagons, as did James Reed and his daughter Virginia. Altogether the three men hired eight hands to act as helpers and teamsters. Reed also hired a young woman, Eliza Williams, to prepare meals, do laundry, and care for Reed's ailing wife and her mother. The older children in the train were also expected to help whenever they could.

Shortly after reaching Independence, the Donner group joined forces with another California-bound family. The parents were Peggy and Patrick Breen. Natives of Ireland, they were about forty years old. Their seven children ranged in age from one to fourteen. Like the Donners, the Breens had three wagons. With them was an Irish friend named Patrick Dolan, a young bachelor. He had one wagon.

When the enlarged group heard that still more people bound for California were moving along the trail ahead of them, they hurried to catch up. Unhappily, the region's spring thunderstorms were sweeping the area. One traveler grumbled that a person couldn't lie down for fear of drowning or stand up for fear of being struck by lightning. The wayfarers could not cross some of the bog holes they encountered until they had cut down small trees and big bushes and had spread a thick, ragged pavement of branches across the mud. Steep stream banks were so slippery that sometimes they had to use two teams to get a wagon up, a process called double teaming.

Riders without wagons to delay them occasionally rode past the Donners. From one of these men they learned that the United States and Mexico had declared war. The information was not really surprising, but it did make the emigrants wonder again about what might be happening in California. But no one was frightened into turning back. On May 19, the Donners caught up with the California group—fifty wagons—that had been ahead of them. And still more wagons, most bound for Oregon, had gotten even farther ahead. Those headed for California, in short, were almost the last emigrants in that year's long, scattered line of movers.

In spite of that, the laggards didn't hurry. When the sun shone again, they took time out to enjoy the warmth and dry their clothes and bedding. Grandmother Keyes, though, was already worn out by age, sickness, and the jolting travel. She died on May 29. (There would be other casualties later on, but of course the Donners didn't know that . . . yet.) The train delayed a full day while the men cut down a tree, built a coffin, and buried her. The pace, however, did not pick up much when the wagons began to roll once more.

The slowness worried a newspaperman named Edwin

Bryant. In his notes he wrote, "I am . . . fearful the winter will find us in the snowy mountains of California."

After publishing his guidebook, in Cincinnati, Lansford Hastings started back toward California. He left Independence, Missouri, on August 17, 1845. With him were ten young men on horseback. They carried their supplies on pack mules. The season was too late for Hastings to look for his shortcut. So his party swung around by Fort Hall. They reached the Sierra Nevada in December. They were lucky. Snow came much later than usual that year.

Although actual war was still several months away, the few Americans already in California were frightened. Suppose the Mexican authorities tried to drive them out. How could they get help in resisting them?

Their fears gave Hastings an idea. As soon as spring came, he would return east over the mountains. He would find his shortcut at last. Having located it, he would continue on past Great Salt Lake to the pass, called South Pass, where westbound trails crossed the Continental Divide. There he would meet the emigrant trains traveling toward Oregon and California. By promising an easy shortcut, he would persuade as many Oregonians as possible to change their minds and accompany him to California. There he would form an illegal army. Without waiting for the United States to declare war, he would attack and drive the small Mexican army back to Mexico. He would then form an independent Pacific Republic with himself as president.

He began his eastbound trip in April, 1846. With him

were eighteen men, two women, and two children. For one reason and another, they were returning to what they called the States. Among them was an old mountaineer named James Clyman. Clyman thought Hastings was a little crazy.

A lot of snow had fallen since Christmas. They had to wait for the warm spring sun to melt some of it out of their way. On the last day of April they crossed the main ridge of the Sierra. Early in May they dropped down into the foothills. At about the time that the Donners and Reeds reached Independence, the Hastings group, bound eastward, pushed into the Nevada desert, poking around for something they could call a shortcut. Word that war had been declared did not reach them.

III

Strange Country

Approximately 670 miles separated Independence from Fort Laramie, a famous Indian trading post in what is now southeastern Wyoming. Traveling those miles took the emigrants from a world of gentle greenness into harsh wastes of sand, broken hills, and patches of grisly white alkali.

Climate created the differences. In Illinois and Missouri frequent snow and rainstorms turned the atmosphere humid. Damp, fertile soil supported oaks and elm and hickory. Grass grew soft and tall on the prairies, as the broad openings in the forests were called.

Farther west the climate turned dry. Infrequent rains took the form of violent electric storms. The flash floods that roared down the ravines quickly sank into the hot sands on the flats. Most of the trees were cottonwoods that found insecure footing on islands in the broad Platte River or formed a ruff along its banks. The sun shone fiercely in air as clear as crystal. Eyes were inflamed by alkali dust. Skin felt parched. Lips cracked.

The very strangeness of this vast new land brought a

sense of adventure to the emigrants. So much to see and learn about! Ordinary grass, for instance. Out here it was curly and brown and grew close to the ground. It looked blighted, and yet it nourished huge herds of buffalo and antelope. The travelers were also amused by the thousands of little prairie dogs (actually a kind of ground squirrel) that stood straight as soldiers on the mounds of earth that circled their burrows. They barked shrill warnings to each other whenever danger appeared.

Mirages were amazing. So were the bluffs lining the south sides of the Platte River Valley near Fort Laramie. Spires, domes, pillars, turrets—you could see almost any shape you wanted. And then, when evening came, you

Many of the travelers tried to climb Chimney Rock, rearing skyward out of the Platte River Valley in present-day Nebraska.
Huntington Library, J. Goldsborough Bruff, artist

went out onto the woodless plain and gathered sacksful of dried pieces of buffalo manure. Relatively small amounts burned hot enough to cook dinner. Sitting around the embers afterward and talking about these wonders helped pull the people together.

But there were also quarrels and misunderstandings that pulled them apart. The hard work of the trail created stress. Before sunrise each day, the oxen had to be caught, yoked, and hitched to the wagons. Then as the circled wagons pulled out into a line, a few families always created confusion by being late. If that happened too often, the people involved were likely to be told, impolitely, to get out and find some other caravan to travel with.

Exposure to the frequent rains at the start of the trip brought on sickness. So did drinking bad water. Caring for the invalids inside overloaded wagons was hard, but when the people doing the nursing begged for a rest, the train's captains, anxious to make good time, often refused. Weariness suddenly turned small problems into big ones. Teamsters would all at once cruelly beat their stubborn oxen. Arguments arose over dogs that barked all night. Hoggish teamsters angered others by trying to push ahead of them in the line.

Occasionally there were fistfights or even knife fights. Friends of the fighters would take sides, yelling and insulting each other. For such reasons—or sometimes for no reason, it seemed—feuds developed. Then a few wagons would pull out of the group they had started with and join another train. It was that way with the big train the Donners, Reeds, and Breens had joined in Kansas. Many left that train, but the Donners, Reeds, and Breens stayed together. Because they seemed dependable, a few additional families gathered around them.

⋆On June 23 they reached the only major resting place on the trail. This was a stretch of land seven or eight miles long between a small fort called Fort Bernard on the east and the Indian trading post, Fort Laramie, on the west. Laramie consisted of strong walls of adobe bricks built around an inside plaza. There were gun turrets at diagonally opposite corners of the building. Massive gates guarded the entrance.

Fort Laramie, first an Indian trading post and later an army installation in southeastern Wyoming, was famous as a place where travelers could rest themselves and their animals, buy supplies, and pick up news. Huntington Library, J. Goldsborough Bruff, artist

Scores of white-topped emigrant wagons and the herds of livestock that had arrived with them dotted the meadows between the two forts. Closer to Laramie and off to one side were the conical tipis of about three thousand Sioux Indians—men, women, and children. Edwin Bryant, who had come this far with the Donners, wrote that many of the Indian women were very beautiful. The great crowd had come to Fort Laramie to buy supplies for a war against enemy tribes.

Shortly after the Donners arrived, hundreds of the Sioux performed a war dance. Drums beat, voices chanted. Their skins painted in designs, the men leaped and wailed and brandished their weapons to show what they were going to do to their foe. The women, their ornaments jingling, were just as excited. The affair was a kind of farewell ceremony. The next day the Indians wove ribbons and feathers into the manes and tails of the horses. Mounting, they formed a parade line about three miles long. Its purpose was to take the women and children to a place where they would be safe during the coming battles. (As events developed, there was no fighting that year.)

The Donners enjoyed the opportunity to rest their oxen, buy a few items they needed at the fort, and watch the Indian performance, which was unlike anything they had seen before. They felt good, too, about their westward progress. They had covered the 670 miles from Independence in forty-five days. Not bad, they told each other.

Edwin Bryant disagreed. He still thought the wagons moved too slowly. To quicken the journey, he and six friends decided to trade their wagons for seven fast-stepping

The Donner Party shared Fort Laramie with a large party of Indians preparing for war against another tribe. Many of the warriors looked like this one. As events turned out, there was no war. NATIONAL PARK SERVICE, RICHARD SCHLECHT, ARTIST

pack mules and pack saddles. None of the men had families. All would be riding horseback. If they could buy additional provisions at Fort Bridger on the west side of the Continental Divide, they ought to reach California in record time.

Just as they were getting started, four men, one woman, and one boy rode into Fort Laramie fresh from California. The leader of the little party was the gaunt, grizzled trapper, James Clyman. Westbound emigrants crowded around him to ask questions about the Mexican province and, especially, about the Hastings shortcut.

Several of the question-askers kept notes on what Clyman said. One was Edwin Bryant, who wanted to get some idea of how long it would take mules to make the crossing. Another of the seekers for information was Heinrich Lienhard. Although Lienhard was traveling with wagons, in a different company from the Donners, his group also intended to try the shortcut.

Both men were surprised by the way Clyman ran down California. A terrible place! He was so extreme in his statements that both Bryant and Lienhard decided he had some private motive for talking as he did. In the end neither of them trusted him.

Clyman also talked to James Frazier Reed. The two men knew each other from having fought Indians together in Iowa many years before. When Reed asked about the shortcut, Clyman said the emigrants should stay away from it no matter what they heard from anyone else.

Reed knew that Clyman was a respected person. Yet he, too, began doubting his old friend. After all, Hastings had offered readers everywhere a printed book that praised California to the skies. It couldn't be all lies, could it? Reed also reminded the group that they'd had their troubles coming 670 miles from Independence. California lay another 1,400 miles away. They were tough miles, the people at the fort said. Any shortcut that would save distance through country like that deserved consideration.

The group discussed the problem thoroughly. They simply couldn't figure out why Clyman had talked the way he did. The doubts made the difference, and they decided to go ahead as they had originally planned—across the shortcut.

After crossing the Sierra Nevada, the Hastings party of eighteen men, two women, and two children had ridden three hundred miles eastward along the great curve of the Humboldt River in present-day Nevada. It was desolate country, ribbed with volcanic mountains, splotched with alkali, almost bare of vegetation, and cold enough, at that time of year, to freeze water every night.

A short distance southwest of present-day Elko, Nevada, the Hastings party split. The larger section wanted to continue along the regular road to Fort Hall. Somehow they had heard that the Indians farther east were on the warpath, and they hoped they could find other eastbound travelers at the fort they could join with for greater safety.

This didn't suit Hastings. He wanted the group to stay together and examine the shortcut that lay ahead. Most of the travelers refused. The land they had crossed had been rough enough, and the supposed shortcut Hastings kept talking about might be worse. Clyman, too, thought the idea was foolish, but he and a few others finally agreed to accompany Hastings.

Tough going! By the time Hastings and his few followers had broken through the jumble of canyons and mountains in northern Utah, their supplies were low. They hoped to get more at ramshackle Fort Bridger, in the southwestern corner of Wyoming. But no one was at the fort. Hungry and fearful of Indians (a false alarm as matters developed), they wandered on toward the Oregon Trail, hoping to meet Jim

Bridger bringing in a stock of fresh supplies for his post. To their astonishment, they met instead some of their former trail mates. No eastbound Oregonians had been at Fort Hall. So now what? Some had decided to stay at Fort Hall. The rest rode on toward Fort Bridger, hoping to find help there. What turned up instead was a part of the Hastings-Clyman group, who had separated from them at the Humboldt River. Clearly going by the shortcut didn't help very much.

In the end Hastings decided to camp near the forks in the trail—Oregon to the northwest, his California shortcut to the southwest. At that strategic spot he would try to lure as many Oregon wagons into his fold as he could. And there Clyman left him. The trapper was sick of the whole business. Hastings, he had decided, was not only foolish, but dangerously so. With just three men, one woman, and one child—easy pickings for a war party!—Clyman started for Independence. Traveling cautiously and living on game, the party reached Laramie shortly after the Donner group had.

Clyman told them and several others exactly what he thought of California and the Hastings shortcut. But they thought he was exaggerating. Realizing they didn't believe him, he gave up the effort and rode on.

Meanwhile, Hastings sat like a spider in his camp at the forks of the trail, waiting for recruits.

IV

Continental Divide

While their oxen grazed and rested on the meadows around Fort Laramie, the large party the Donners were with worked at repairing their wagons, cleaning their clothes and equipment, and packing the fresh supplies they had bought. During this period many of the other trains that had paused at the fort began slowly creaking westward. Soon it became clear that the Donner group and their traveling companions would be among the last to resume their long journey. Clearly, those bound for California had let the thought of a shortcut make them overconfident.

They could see their first major obstacle from the top of the bluffs overlooking the fort. These were the Black Hills. From a distance they looked low and harmless. Their dark appearance came from the thin forests of gnarled junipers and stunted pine trees that covered them. (Today the hills are called the Laramie Range. The name Black Hills has migrated 150 miles north to another set of small mountains in western South Dakota.)

The North Platte River followed a rough canyon around the northern part of the Laramie Range. Unfortunately, wagons could not push through that canyon. Instead the emigrants had to climb, with exasperating toil, onto uplands far back from the river. Ahead of them a series of tributary streams ran from south to north, to join the main river. The streams were small but they had cut deep gashes into the uplands. The wagons had to dive down into each of those boulder-choked ravines and then struggle out again.

After several days of this, they came once more to the North Platte River. It was a moment of farewell. The stream that had led them westward for scores of miles bent abruptly to the south. To continue their journey west the emigrants would have to cross it.

The Donner Party probably used the same method as shown below to ferry their wagons and oxen (not mules, as in the illustration) across the North Platte River on the Oregon Trail. HUNTINGTON LIBRARY, J. GOLDSBOROUGH BRUFF, ARTIST

Near the present town of Casper, Wyoming, they either appropriated a raft that had been left on the far bank by an earlier party, or they built a new one out of driftwood and pine logs cut down with axes in the nearby forest. The clumsy ferry could carry only a single wagon at a time. Back and forth, back and forth, they went, laboring with long, homemade sweep oars assisted by windlasses set up on each bank. The several hundred head of livestock that accompanied the caravan had to be driven across the icy current by yelling, whip-swinging riders—an exciting show for the watching women and children.

Their labors brought them belatedly into a wasteland of weird rock formations, gritty hills, and small streams and ponds poisonous with alkali. They carefully skirted bog holes big enough, in some cases, to mire livestock. Many of the nauseous pits stank of sulfur compounds. Mosquitoes tormented both people and animals. Most of the fifty-mile stretch was dry as powder. Hoofs and wheels churned up eye-stinging clouds of dust. Cooks had to use scrawny chunks of sagebrush and greasewood for fuel. But at least there was pretty good grass near the little streams for the livestock.

This miserable stretch ended at a stream so clear, cold, and pure that trappers long ago had named it Sweetwater Creek. Rising out of the nearby flats was a swaybacked oval of gray-brown granite about a mile in circumference and two hundred feet high. Called Independence Rock, it was the most famous landmark on the trail. Like hundreds of people before them and thousands who would come later, the Donners and their friends painted or used chisels to leave their names as high up its scabby surface as they could get.

This broader view of Independence Rock also shows Sweetwater River. Its valley was followed by west-bound immigrants almost as far as the Continental Divide. The Continental Divide is an imaginary line that runs the length of the Rocky Mountains separating rivers that flow in an easterly direction from those that flow in a westerly direction. Scott's Bluff National Monument, William Henry Jackson, artist

Many immigrants, including some from the Donner Party, either chiseled or painted their names on the granite of Independence Rock in what is now central Wyoming. Stephen Trimble, photographer

Then on again, step by step by step. They passed a huge cleft called Devil's Gate. Gradually the granite walls of the valley shrank into a vast sage plain. Off to the right rose the towering, snowcapped peaks of the Wind River Mountains. Thank heavens they didn't have to cross them!

Somewhere along the Sweetwater they encountered a lone rider named Bonney. He carried a message written by Lansford Hastings and directed to all California emigrants. The creased piece of paper told again about the marvelous shortcut. Bonney, who had spoken to Hastings, added that the promoter was now waiting at Fort Bridger for a few last recruits.

Arguments flared up again in the train the Donners were with. Bonney said he knew nothing about the shortcut. He had ridden alone from Fort Hall to Sweetwater Creek. Alone! Obviously the route was a good one. Some of the emigrants changed their minds again. They'd go by Fort Hall.

The Donners, James Reed, and the Breens, and others stayed firm. Surely the shortest route would be the quickest. Also, they wanted to stop at Fort Bridger. There Reed could replace the four oxen that had died from drinking poison alkali water. They could use the fort's blacksmith shop to reset the iron tires on their wagons and put new shoes on the sore feet of the oxen. George Donner could hire a new teamster to take the place of Hiram Miller. Miller had joined Edwin Bryant's small party of horsemen near Fort Laramie, and his services were sorely missed. Best of all, they could rest themselves and their livestock for a few days.

Talking so, they reached the Continental Divide at South

Pass. It was not the narrow ridge they had expected. It was just a slight rise on a broad plain spotted with sagebrush. Sagebrush and a vast emptiness! It was July 18, and they still had at least a thousand more miles to cover. Some of the women with small children must have shivered at the thought. How glad they were that Hastings had found a quicker way across that cruel land!

The actual separation took place at Little Sandy Creek, a few miles west of South Pass. There twenty wagons left the train and swung southwest. With them they carried the hopes and skimpy possessions of eight families, a scattering of single men, and a forlorn waif named Luke Halloran— seventy-one people altogether. George Donner was elected captain of the group.

They had found Halloran huddled in a wretched little shelter of willows and canvas close to the Little Sandy. He had been with a party of horsemen but had become so sick he could not keep up. Unable to carry him along, his companions had left him beside the trail in the hope that some compassionate wagon master would come along and agree to carry him on toward the coast, if indeed he lived that long. When the Donner train appeared, he approached the new captain and begged for a ride. George nodded. They made a bed for Luke in one of the new captain's three wagons. George's wife, Tamsen, a tiny woman hardly five feet tall, undertook to be his nurse.

At the time of separation, one of the emigrants bound toward Oregon wrote that of those seventy-one people Tamsen alone looked as if she feared what lay ahead.

Modern wheel tracks lead to South Pass. The pass was one of the few places where the Continental Divide could be crossed by wagons. The Donners left the Oregon Trail a few miles west of the Divide on their way to Hastings Cutoff. STEPHEN TRIMBLE, PHOTOGRAPHER

Sixty-six wagons (by one count) had reached Fort Bridger ahead of George Donner's group. Circles of their white-topped vehicles took shape in every direction. Even more numerous were the tipis of visiting Indians and of the many traders who had arrived to do business with the emigrants.

It was a lively scene, Edwin Bryant admitted, when he

Fort Bridger was the last inhabited spot where travelers could rest and replace worn-out oxen with fresh stock. STEPHEN TRIMBLE, PHOTOGRAPHER

and his riders jogged into the valley. But after he had talked to Lansford Hastings and an old mountain man he met there, he began to wonder whether heavy wagons pulled by long strings of oxen really could be taken through the mountains that loomed ahead. He wrote a letter of warning to James Reed and entrusted it to Louis Vasquez, one of the owner's of the fort, for delivery. Having no wagons themselves, Bryant and his companions then set out to cross the shortcut with saddle animals. With them went scouts dispatched by Hastings to look for a better route through the Wasatch Mountains of Utah than he and Clyman and their companions had followed on their journey east. Another route! That in itself was enough to make a person wonder.

Meanwhile the emigrants camped at Fort Bridger were growing impatient. Time was slipping by. They should be on the move!

Hastings agreed. Without making any effort to learn whether more wagons were still rumbling along the trail from the Little Sandy, he gave the order to start.

After all, latecomers, if there were any, should be able to follow the tracks left by sixty-six wagons. Shouldn't they?

V

Worse and Worse the Way

The veteran trappers, Jim Bridger and Louis Vasquez, suspected that the mountains and the hideous salt desert southwest of their fort could be a nightmare for travelers. But they had only seen the edges of the area. So when Hastings told them he'd found a passable trail, they believed him.

It suited their purposes to do so. If a good shortcut existed, a lot of wagons carrying a lot of potential customers would go past their trading post. Accordingly, they told the Donners the route was worth trying. True, the desert was forty miles wide, but if the emigrants filled their water casks and carried along bundles of grass for their oxen, they could push through by driving one day and one night without sleep. During this talk Louis Vasquez did not say a word about the letter Edwin Bryant had given him to deliver to Jim Reed—a letter warning the emigrants *not* to take the shortcut.

For four restful days they hung around the post. George Donner hired a young roustabout from New Mexico, Jean Baptiste Trubode, to serve as teamster and help with the livestock. A kindly man, George also took pity on three more waifs, the William McCutchen family. The father was a massive man, six feet six inches tall, with a great chest. He and his young wife, Amanda, were the parents of a year-old baby girl. William's wagon had been wrecked beyond repair, and he was unable to find another he could afford. The gentle captain of the train said not to worry. They'd crowd the McCutchens in somehow. The addition meant that there were now five nursing babies in the train—and twenty-six children twelve years or younger.

Their twenty wagons left Fort Bridger on July 31. Although the sixty-six wagons ahead of them had smoothed out the worst places in the trail, travel was still a bone-jarring experience, and the loose cattle were hard to keep moving ahead in the thick brush. After a week of this,

Big, husky William McCutchen, his wife Amanda, and their year-old daughter Harriet joined the Donner Party at Fort Bridger. HUNTINGTON LIBRARY

they reached a pretty mountain meadow through which the Weber River flowed.

There they found a note from Hastings attached to a bush. It was directed to whoever might be following him. In it he said he was trying to improve on his shortcut by leading his big train through the canyon of the Weber to Great Salt Lake. The effort had turned into a nightmare. Whoever was behind him should send a messenger to him. He would then return and guide the latecomers to the better trail James Clyman and he had found when traveling east earlier that year.

Three messengers from the Donner Party did overtake the Hastings group. Hastings, however, would not come back as he had promised. He said his first responsibility was to his own train. The most he would do was accompany one of the messengers, James Reed, to a nearby peak top. From there he pointed toward high ridges and saddles, dim in the distance. Over there, he said, was where the trail ran.

Perhaps the Donners should have tried going through the canyon of the Weber. The sixty-six wagons that had just traveled it must have improved the road somewhat. But Reed, who had also seen the canyon, said travel there remained highly dangerous. The Hastings people had smashed one wagon to smithereens and had hurt several oxen during their journey. So once again the Donners accepted Lansford Hastings' advice about routes.

Making trail as they went, they broke a passageway into a maze of peaks, hogback ridges, twisting canyons, and swampy hollows. Using their axes, they chopped a way through tangled mats of small trees and brush. Heaving on their crowbars, they pried boulders out of the way. With picks and shovels, they leveled off the approaches to deep, narrow ravines. They couldn't pull their wagons into a group at night but left them strung out along the new roadway. Such open space as there was, they had to share with the bewildered cattle and horses.

On the third day a shout rang out. Up came ''Uncle Billy'' Graves, aged fifty-seven, with three wagons and the thirteen members of his family, including two married daughters. On hearing that the Donners were not far ahead of them on the shortcut, they had left their original train and had hurried to catch up. Their arrival brought the number

Big Mountain, in effect the beginning of the Hastings Cutoff, proved to be almost impenetrable by wagons. The Donner group spent twenty days chopping out thirty-six miles of ''road.'' STEPHEN TRIMBLE, PHOTOGRAPHER

of children under twelve to twenty-nine. One was another nursing baby. Altogether there were now eighty-seven people in the Donner Party.

Among the newcomers were four strong, young grown-ups. But even with their help, the caravan often traveled no more than a mile or a mile and a half between dawn and dark. Every worker ached from bruised muscles, blistered hands, twisted backs, and scratched and bleeding faces. Quarrels flared up. The women, too, grew cranky from keeping watch over the restless children, cooking meals in difficult places, and patching up injuries. Was this what they had left home for?

After three laborious weeks, all twenty-three wagons reached the plains that curved around the southern shore of Great Salt Lake. Both the weary people and the weary

Pilot Peak loomed like a beacon on the far side of Utah's Bonneville Salt Flats, as they are known today. Although the Donners lost several wagons and oxen during the crossing, all the humans survived. STEPHEN TRIMBLE, PHOTOGRAPHER

animals needed rest. Yet they dared not stop. It was August 27. And California's Sierra Nevada—Spanish words that mean snowy mountains—were still hundreds of miles away.

Luke Halloran, the sick young man Tamsen Donner had been nursing, died within sight of the lead-colored inland sea. Pushing on after burying him, the migrants again picked up the tracks of Hastings' sixty-six wagons. It was clear now that the big train was many days ahead of them. A tall, handsome, bearded man named Lewis Keseberg began finding fault with James Reed for having picked the wrong route. Others echoed him, and angry words flashed back and forth.

It was a poor time for quarreling. On September 1, in a place called Skull Valley, they reached several springs of clear, cold water. They also found a note on a piece of torn paper. It said that crossing the dry desert ahead of them would take two full days and nights—twice as long as they had been told at Bridger's Fort.

The men spent the next day desperately cutting the grass that grew around the springs. This they stuffed into what empty spaces there were inside the loaded wagons. It was the only food the oxen would have during the crossing of the desert. The women prepared carry-along meals for the families. They filled every pot and bucket that would hold water. Then on September 3 they started.

The sun beat down from a sky so blue it seemed enameled. The cold nights took on a weird beauty under the ghostly light of a full moon. Unexpected mountains thrust up from the desert floor and had to be crossed. Sand dunes dragged at hoofs and wheels. Two days passed. Two nights. No end was in sight.

Warned that an utterly barren desert lay beyond a spring like this one, the Donner Party frantically collected water and cut grass they could carry in their wagons. They supposed the journey would take two days and two nights. It dragged out to six. STEPHEN TRIMBLE, PHOTOGRAPHER

On the third day the most heavily loaded wagons—those of the Donners and Jim Reed among them—fell behind. Lighter outfits pulled ahead. Each family unit was concerned only with itself. Soon vehicles, loose livestock, and people were scattered out across several miles. The oxen sucked up the last water in the buckets, ate the last bundles of grass. Four days. The faltering animals could not pull the wagons. The men unhitched them and drove them ahead, hoping to find water. After the cattle had rested for a few hours, they would return for the wagons.

Several of the terrified women stayed with the vehicles. Other, younger ones, who were used to walking along the trail, started walking along the wheel tracks. Some carried babies while urging the older children to keep moving. Five days. Walkers began staggering through the willows that fringed a blessed spring.

The men scattered out. Some drove their ox teams back to the wagons to rescue the waiting women and children and the walkers who had not yet arrived. Other men searched for the strayed livestock.

Miraculously not a human life had been lost. But many animals either perished or vanished. No effort was made by the people in the train to share the losses. Each owner had to bear his own misfortune. Reed, the richest man in the caravan, lost so many oxen that he had to abandon two of his wagons. To salvage as many of his possessions as he could, he kept the big, top-heavy vehicle he had built for his wife's mother, who had died back in Kansas. But the four oxen he still owned could scarcely move it. So he strengthened the team by buying one ox and one cow from a luckier emigrant. He was not the only sufferer. George Donner and Lewis Keseberg each had to leave a loaded wagon behind.

They couldn't afford to rest—but they had to. On the point of collapsing from weariness, they halted at the next spring, only a few miles away. As strength began to return to the oxen and themselves, a new terror hit them. There was not enough food left in the wagons to carry them to California.

What could be done? They couldn't hurry. Yet they had to keep moving west as best they could. So there wasn't much point in sending an appeal to Fort Bridger. Its supplies were limited, anyway. The only hope was for someone to ride ahead, cross the Sierra Nevada, and buy as much as possible from Sutter's Fort in California's Sacramento Valley.

Who should go?

Who could be counted on to come back after escaping this dreadful trap in the desert?

Big William McCutchen volunteered. His wife and baby agreed to stay with the train. Saving them would guarantee his return.

Other women in the train did not want their husbands leaving them and their children. So Charles Stanton said he'd go with McCutchen. Stanton was a bachelor. He was a foot shorter than McCutchen. But he had already proved himself to be strong, capable, and trustworthy. He was chosen immediately.

By the time the two left, the train was moving again. They continued following the tracks of Hastings' sixty-six wagons. The big caravan, they soon noticed, wavered strangely. Someone finally guessed why. While traveling east earlier in the year, the Hastings-Clyman explorers had been riding horses. Wagons, however, couldn't cross many of the places that had caused the horses little trouble. Now Hastings was searching for a way by which wagons could cross the tall Ruby Mountains that ran north and south just ahead of them. His choice of routes led far south. In dragging after him, the Donners were wasting time getting practically nowhere. But they didn't know what else to do.

At last they found a way through the Ruby range and turned north. On September 30 they reached the Humboldt River a few miles west of present-day Elko, Nevada. The stream was actually no more than a small creek. But for

Much of the desert travel occurred in eerie moonlight. In the background are the Ruby Mountains as seen from Nevada's Ruby Valley. STEPHEN TRIMBLE, PHOTOGRAPHER

most of its course it followed a southwesterly direction across the entire area of what is now Nevada. Because of its direction and its water, the main trail to California—the one that passed by Fort Hall—clung as close to its banks as the rugged terrain allowed.

The Donners should have rejoiced. Hastings' deadly shortcut was behind them at last! But instead of smiles there were curses. They had saved no time and probably no miles. Because of the failure, they might not reach the Sierra Nevada ahead of the first big snowstorm. Or Mc-Cutchen and Stanton might not be able to reach them with the food they had to have.

Yet what could they do except plod painfully ahead, hoping for the best while expecting the worst.

VI

Snowed In

As September drew toward its end, the pressures on the Donner Party increased. Food was running out. Paiute Indians lurking along the trail stole or killed unwatched animals. Knowing that time was growing short, the people who had the best oxen—the Donner families were among them—began pushing ahead of the others. Those left behind grew alarmed and tried to make their weary animals speed up.

In one tight place, John Snyder, who worked for Uncle Billy Graves, tried to push ahead of a wagon Milt Elliott was driving for James Reed. Both teamsters were, of course, afoot. As the animals of the two teams jostled against each other, Snyder began beating them furiously with his heavy bullwhip. Reed rushed over to stop him. Snyder lashed at him, cutting his face badly. When Mrs. Reed tried to interfere, he struck her, too. At that, Reed drew his knife and stabbed Snyder to death.

The horrified people of the rear section of the train formed a council. Keseberg demanded that Reed be hanged. The council chose instead to banish him into the desert with one bony horse but no gun. In effect they were saying to let the Indians finish him. Rather than cause more dissension, the repentant Reed accepted the harsh punishment. His friends, William Eddy and Milt Elliott, promised to take care of his family. Just before he rode away, someone, perhaps his daughter Virginia, smuggled a rifle to him.

A day's ride brought him to the front of the caravan. The people there were more sympathetic. They gave him a little food from their meager stores. And another of his teamsters, Walter Herron, who no longer had a wagon to drive, agreed to go with him. Herron had no horse, however, and so for a time the two men had to take turns riding Reed's sorry-looking mount. The horse soon played out, and they abandoned it.

Meanwhile the situation back at the train blurred into horror. First there was the elderly man known in the records only as Hardkoop. He was nearly seventy and had no family with him. At the start of the trip, he had paid Lewis Keseberg to carry his few possessions as he walked. Along the Humboldt he grew too feeble to continue on foot. Keseberg let him ride in one of his wagons for a while. But the extra weight hurt the oxen. Noticing this, Keseberg ordered Hardkoop to get out. No other wagon would take him in. No one would lend him a horse. Even if George Donner had tried, as captain, to interfere, no one would have heeded him. The whole party was demoralized and sullen. Hardkoop dropped behind and was never seen again.

The Paiutes kept shooting arrows at the animals. They easily eluded the whites' disorganized efforts at striking back. So many oxen were killed that a few more wagons had to be abandoned. One belonged to a man named Wolfinger. Unable to carry his and his wife's favorite possessions, he decided to dig a hole in the dry ground and cache (hide) the goods. Later he would return for them.

Rather than stay behind with him while he worked, his wife continued walking with some of the other women. Two men, Joseph Reinhardt and Augustus Spitzer, dropped back, saying they would help Wolfinger. A few days later they rejoined the train without him. They said Indians had killed him. Later there were whispers that the whites themselves had killed the helpless man for the money he carried in a belt around his waist.

No one investigated. The people were too tired. But George Donner, always compassionate, made room for the grief-stricken widow in one of his remaining vehicles.

Twelve days after first reaching the Humboldt, the travelers came to the huge marsh—they called it a "sink"—into which the river oozed and died. The grass around the seep was sparse. The water was hardly drinkable. There were ridges of sand to labor across and springs of boiling hot water to avoid. Bog holes made the margins of the sink dangerous. A horse belonging to Patrick Breen mired itself in one and died when no one would help Breen pull it out.

Beyond the sink stretched another forty-mile stretch of waterless desert. But at least they knew that on its far side they would meet the clear, cold, sparkling Truckee River, named for the leader of a band of Indians. This was the river that would take them most of the way to the crest of the Sierra Nevada. Beyond the crest lay the wide, warm, beautiful valleys of California. If they could reach the river, and if Stanton and McCutchen showed up with more food, they could hope again.

The prospect did not make the group more cooperative. By then, only fifteen of the original twenty-three wagons remained. Their owners would not share an inch of space with those who had no vehicles. They feared that every extra pound was a threat. In fact, most of the owners lightened the loads in their vehicles by throwing away some of their heaviest possessions.

No one waited for anyone else. As soon as a family was ready, off it went. Perhaps the cruelest moment came when Eddy was carrying his infant daughter in his arms while fiercely urging his wife and their three-year-old son to keep walking. They were all gasping for water. Breen, who still had a little in a cask attached to his wagon, refused to give them any. Furious, Eddy forced him at gunpoint to part with a few swallows.

Small in size but great in courage, Charles Stanton, accompanied by Big Bill McCutchen, rode ahead of the main group to Sutter's Fort in California. They wanted to bring back food for their companions. McCutchen fell ill at the fort. Helped by two Indians, Stanton rode back across the Sierra with seven muleloads of provisions—too little and too late. HUNTINGTON LIBRARY

Demoralized though it was, the entire party reached the Truckee River without loss of life. Shade, water—and then a morsel of food. Eddy went hunting and came back with nine fat geese. They were thin pickings when spread among eighty people. Yet the smell of them roasting brought a little cheer. A happier moment followed the killing of an ox by the Paiutes. The whites were able to drive the Indians away and butcher the animal for their own use.

Still traveling in widely separated sections, they toiled up the rocky canyon of the Truckee. On the third day, the miracle they had been praying for occurred—on a limited scale. The first wagon met Charles Stanton and two Indians driving seven head of pack mules loaded with flour and dried beef. All had been furnished by John Augustus Sutter at his trading post in California's Sacramento Valley. The Indians had Spanish names, Luis and Salvador. They had helped Stanton pack and unpack the mules at each night's camp.

While the excited emigrants watched, the rescuers unpacked three of the mules. The rest they took down the canyon to the second section. After the food had been distributed, the weariest of the women and children were able to ride the mules.

On reaching the broad Truckee Meadows (the city of Reno, Nevada, stands there today), the train pulled together again. Stanton answered a barrage of questions. Mc-Cutchen had fallen sick, and Stanton had not dared wait for him to recover before heading back to the wagons with as many mules as he and the two Indians could handle. Reed and Herron? Yes, they'd gotten across. They hadn't taken time to hunt because they wanted to reach Sutter's, buy provisions, and return to the train before snow came. As a result they had nearly starved. Stanton was sure that as soon as they recovered, they, too, would start back with supplies.

And then Stanton made a deadly mistake. Frontiersmen at Sutter's Fort had assured him that big snows seldom blanketed the mountains before the middle of November. There might be small snowfalls before then, but a day or two of sunlight would quickly melt them.

With those assurances in mind, Stanton carefully looked over the milling group. Every person and work ox he saw was in poor physical shape. A few days' rest would boost their chances of climbing the rugged granite slopes that led to the pass. Why not take the chance? It was October 20. Three weeks remained before truly big storms could be expected.

He assembled the adults in the party and asked for their votes. Every one of them agreed to stop awhile and rest.

The next day William Pike, twenty-five years old and the father of two small children, was killed in a gun accident.

A shiver of dread ran through the people as they buried him. Was there no end? Some of them counted up the fatalities that had occurred since they had chosen this next-to-impossible route. Halloran, Hardkoop, Snyder, Wolfinger, and now William Pike. Three more whose strength was sadly missed—McCutchen, Reed, and Herron—were somewhere off beyond the mountains. Seventy-nine remained. They could hardly help wondering, there in that crushing isolation, who might be next.

Yet even after resting, they would not stay together. When they left the meadows on October 25 or so, they traveled in three ragged sections, according to the strength of their oxen and the milk cows that were also yoked. Clouds lowered over the mountaintops and spits of snow stung their faces.

Stanton was with the second group, but he gave the first one careful directions. Several miles up the mountain, the valley of the Truckee bent south. The emigrants should continue west up to Alder Creek and then cross south over a low ridge to a glistening lake. Just beyond the lake rose the steep cliffs that guarded the pass. On October 31, this first group—the Breens, the Eddys, the Kesebergs, and Patrick Dolan—reached the heavily forested valley that cupped what was then called Truckee Lake (now it is Donner Lake). About a quarter of a mile below the lake was a small log cabin that had been built by an earlier party. Breen was the first to see the cabin. The point would become important later on.

They camped close by. Snow was falling and some of it was sticking to the ground. The storm continued the next morning. Terror rippled through them as they worked a way around the lake's north shore. As they climbed higher, the snow grew deeper and drier. Finally the oxen could no longer drag the wagons ahead. The emigrants turned back to the cabin. Breen claimed the right to occupy it because he was the first to have seen it.

That night and all the next day cold rain fell. With renewed hope the campers told each other that so much rain would surely wash away most of the snow.

At dark the second section dragged in. Stanton and Sutter's two Indian workers were with them. There was no sign of the Donners.

Unable to cross the Sierra because of snow, the main group of travelers hastily built shelters in which to wait out the storms. From an old drawing made from description furnished by William G. Murphy. HUNTINGTON LIBRARY

By dawn the skies were clear again. Through the trunks of the tall pines, they could see the awesome wall that blocked the way to the pass. Except for dark bands of granite too steep for snow to cling to, it glistened pure white. No trail was visible. Stanton, though, had crossed the barrier twice. He thought he could find the way again. A few of the people were so worn out they refused to go with him. They'd rather wait for help to reach them from the outside, they said. Most, however, yoked their creaky wagons and edged past the lake once more. Soon they were floundering in huge drifts. What had been rain at the lake had been snow at higher elevations.

Late in the day, they decided to abandon the wagons. They cinched packs of bedding and their small amounts of food on the backs of the rebellious cattle. While some carried the smallest children, the rest drove the oxen ahead. It was a hopeless effort. Stanton and the two Indians, struggling ahead with the mules, could not break out a trail. At dark they quit trying, set fire to a tall, dead pine, and made beds out of blankets for the children. The rest huddled as close to the fire as they could.

More snow fell during the night. When the thin light of dawn came, they saw that some of the oxen had wandered away. Without trying to find them, the stranded emigrants turned back toward the lake. They didn't even try to salvage the wagons they had abandoned.

The ground near the cabin claimed by the Breens was flat. Water and wood were handy. Grimly, the travelers began building more small, windowless huts of crooked logs. They made roofs by laying down poles side by side. These they covered with evergreen boughs, spare blankets, and a hide or two. Counting Breen's cabin, sixty people faced the future in four poor huts and a lean-to. Each shelter held a crude fireplace built of rocks.

The Donner brothers, their children, their four teamsters, and Mrs. Wolfinger fared no better. They were stalled beside Alder Creek, about six miles from the lake. A broken axle had caused one of their wagons to collapse flat on its side. Its tumbling load nearly crushed the two children who were riding in it. While the Donners were frantically working on a new axle, George cut his hand severely but did nothing more about the wound than wrap it in an old cloth. As the snowfall increased, they saw they were losing their race with time. They must have shelter. So they

Delayed by a wagon accident, the Donner brothers, their families and their helpers built flimsy shelters in meadows such as this beside Alder Creek. Their camp was about six miles from the one located at what became known as Donner Lake. PATRICE PRESS, CHARLES GRAYDON, PHOTOGRAPHER

erected three tents under the overhanging boughs of big evergreen trees. They covered these with logs, poles, brush, old blankets—anything that might shield them from the snow. The patchwork structures would have to shelter six men (including the Donners' four teamsters), three women, and twelve children.

At the very time the Donner Party was building crude shelters high on the eastern side of the Sierra Nevada, Jim

Reed and Big Bill McCutchen were starting up the western side to meet them. The two men, helped by Indian workers Sutter had loaned them, were driving thirty-one horses ahead of them. Only a part of the herd carried food. The would-be rescuers thought the people had surely pushed across the pass before snow trapped them. Thus their main hope was to bring in riding horses for those who most needed help—the small children, the women, the sick.

They failed. As they rode higher into the mountains, the snow piled deeper. They had to leave more and more of the horses behind. Finally they tried to go ahead on foot. Soon they were sinking into powdery snow up to their chests. They had to turn back.

When Sutter heard their story, he said the unusual depth of the snow probably meant that no human beings would be able to cross the mountains before the last part of February. But, he went on, there was no need worrying. The emigrants surely could butcher enough oxen to keep even eighty people alive for another three and a half or four months.

Neither Sutter nor Reed nor McCutchen realized how few of the caravan's oxen remained alive.

Although not accurate, this artist's rendering suggests the desperation of the travelers as winter closed in on them. COLLECTION OF THE OAKLAND MUSEUM OF CALIFORNIA, THE OAKLAND MUSEUM KAHN COLLECTION, WILLIAM GILBERT GAUL, ARTIST

VII

Desperation

The two segments of the Donner Party built their shelters during a storm that lasted from November 4 to November 11. In that time not much snow accumulated at the lake. The ground still held enough of summer's warmth to melt part of what fell. Spells of rain washed more away. The openness allowed people who were not actively engaged in building shelters to try their hands at hunting and fishing.

The results were alarming. That late in the year, trout in high-altitude lakes won't bite. Animals migrate to lower elevations. William Eddy was the best outdoorsman of the lot. But during three days of strenuous hunting with a single-shot, muzzle-loading rifle, he bagged only one owl and a lean coyote. And by then, the food Stanton and Sutter's two Indians had brought in from California was consumed.

Clearly people could stay alive only by eating their remaining dogs, oxen, and horses. Unfortunately, they had lost most of their animals to the desert, the Indians, and careless herding. Somehow they had to get more help from the outside.

How?

They had already failed twice to cross the pass. But those efforts had been burdened by old people, children, and wagons that had bogged down in the blizzard-driven snow above the lake. However, a small group of sturdy young people traveling without animals might break through and reach the settlements in California. There they could organize a rescue party.

Two more attempts were made. The first group consisted of thirteen men and two women, the daughters of Uncle Billy Graves. The effort failed because of the strange nature of high-altitude snow. Unlike snow in the East, it was as dry and light as talcum powder. In fact, modern skiers call

The summit of the Sierra as seen from the cabins at the lake. The low saddle that was later named Donner Pass is at the right hand part of the photograph. PATRICE PRESS, CHARLES GRAYDON, PHOTOGRAPHER

it "powder snow." At each step, the travelers sank to their hips. At dark they gave up and returned to the cabins. They would have to wait until the snow had settled and the sun had melted its surface. The cold nights would then freeze the top layer into a crust. Held up by the compacted snow underneath, the crust might support their weight.

William Eddy filled the time by hunting. At great risk to himself, he killed a huge grizzly bear that was looking for a place to hibernate. No matter how big the bear was, however, it wouldn't feed several dozen people for long. Realizing this, Eddy's wife hid a small part of their share of the meat. It might help save them if rescue was slow in coming.

For ten days the weather stayed clear. The snow packed down and the adventurers set out again. The party had grown—twenty-two men instead of thirteen, six women instead of two. Stanton, the two Indians, and the mules went first, hoping to smooth out a trail on top of the crusted snow.

The plan was only partly successful. The crust did hold up under the trampling of the people. The mules, however, kept breaking through and then floundered wildly to get out. Their struggles continued even after they had been moved to the packed snow at the end of the column. By the time the hikers had crossed the pass and had pushed a little way down the far side of the mountain, the animals were totally exhausted and could go no farther.

At camp that night, Eddy proposed killing two or three of the animals for food and abandoning the others. Stanton refused. He had promised Sutter on his honor that he would bring the animals back, and he would not break his word. He argued that another two or three days of good weather would strengthen the crust enough to hold the mules as well as the people. So he proposed returning to the shelters at the lake and waiting.

After a miserable night of intense argument, Stanton settled the matter. He had traveled the trail into California twice, once with the two Indians. No one else knew the landmarks they would need to work their way down the mountain. So when Stanton and the Indians started back to the lake with the mules, the others had little choice but to follow.

Instead of the clear weather he had hoped for, another blizzard swept across the pass. For a week the hungry emigrants struggled to get firewood, melt snow to drink, cook their tiny scraps of meat, and stay warm. They did not keep a close watch over the livestock. The last horses, the last oxen, and Sutter's seven mules drifted away, died, and were covered by such deep drifts they could not be found.

Many people were furious with Stanton. They said he should have butchered the mules up on the pass. Then the rescue party could have kept on moving. Instead, he had cost them their best chance for escape. And the mules had died anyway. Stanton did not let the scorn bother him. He and Uncle Billy Graves were working on a plan for overcoming the deep powder snow brought by the latest storm. They would make snowshoes. Both men had once lived in regions of heavy snowfall, Stanton in upper New York State, Graves in Vermont. They knew how snowshoes were made. Now they discovered that the materials needed for making them were at their fingertips. Long, narrow strips of pliant hickory could be cut from the oxbows that locked yokes onto the necks of the work oxen. These pieces of hickory could be warmed and bent into oval frames. Webbing was made by crisscrossing strips of leather cut from an ox's hide.

By the time the two men had run out of materials, they had fashioned twenty-eight of the clumsy objects—fourteen pair. The trouble was, seventeen people wanted to go.

Stanton and Uncle Billy used logic on the problem. They reasoned that fourteen snowshoers traveling single file would pack down a trail strong enough to hold the last three travelers. Choosing the right three was easy. Two young brothers, Lemuel Murphy, aged twelve, and William Murphy, eleven, were real lightweights. A third choice was a skinny, thirty-year-old German teamster named Karl Burger. All three were advised that no one would wait for them if they failed to keep up.

Still other arrangements seem fiercely cruel to modern readers. What, for example, should parents do about small children?

Of the five young women who sought to escape on the snowshoe trips, three entrusted their infants to older women who stayed in the camp. One was Amanda Mc-Cutchen, aged thirty. Her husband, Big Bill McCutchen, was somewhere west of the mountains with Jim Reed—if he was still alive. Wild to find him, she entrusted her year-old baby to the care of Uncle Billy Graves's wife. Another woman without a husband to help her was Harriet Murphy Pike. Her husband had been killed in the gun accident at Truckee Meadows. Numb with grief, she turned her two small girls, aged three and one, over to their grandmother, Lavina Murphy. Harriet's sister, Sarah Murphy Foster, also entrusted her four-year-old to Lavina.

The view from Donner Pass east across the frozen lake. Patrice Press, Charles Graydon, photographer

Perhaps Lavina thought that if the two sisters went with the party, they could look after their two kid brothers, Lemuel and William—the ones without snowshoes.

Three of the men faced similar choices. William Foster decided to go with his wife Sarah rather than help old Mrs. Murphy with the burden of the infants. Uncle Billy Graves chose to go with his two grown daughters, Mary Ann Graves, who was unmarried, and Sarah Graves Fosdick, who had no children. He left the rest of his big family behind in a crowded, stinking shelter. This was a reckless decision. Uncle Billy (whose real name was Franklin Ward Graves) was fifty-seven and considered himself as tough as a Sierra pine. He had accompanied the same two daughters, Mary Ann and Sarah, on the trip that had come to an angry end when Stanton had refused to harm Sutter's seven mules. But that trip had lasted only a day and a night. This one might drag on for . . . well they estimated six days at least.

Then there was William Eddy. He left behind a wife, a three-year-old son, and a year-old daughter.

Another bit of ugliness had to do with food for the trip. They divided what little meat the camp thought it could spare into six small packets, one per day per person. Stanton had trouble getting his share. Yet he was the closest to being a guide they had.

A bachelor, he'd had no oxen to start with. He had paid one of the wagon owners to carry his meager possessions while he rode horseback or walked when necessary. Always willing to help, he had made the long journey to California for food. He had put together some of the snowshoes. But what his companions remembered most in those dark days was his bad advice about loitering at the Truckee Meadows and his refusal to sacrifice Sutter's mules. As a kind of punishment, they ignored his need to provide for the two Indians as well as for himself. When he begged for handouts, the people he approached gave him only the meagerest scraps.

As events developed, the stinginess may have been a serious mistake.

The snowshoers of course hoped to save their own lives. But they also knew that unless they reached civilization and sent back a relief party, everyone in the camp was likely to perish. After all, they had been there forty-six days without adequate food and shelter.

The seriousness of the situation was emphasized the night of December 15, only hours before the snowshoers were to start their journey. Bayliss Williams, one of Reed's teamsters, died of malnutrition and was buried under a mound of snow by his sister, Eliza. (Though the people at the lake didn't yet know it, matters were worse at the Donners' camp on Alder Creek. Four people had died there. Jacob Donner, the oldest member, was one. The other three were single men who just seemed to give up trying to stay alive.)

The morning of December 16 dawned bright and clear. The weather was the only good sign. The fourteen snow-shoers, marching single file, did not pack the snow as

Throughout the dreary days when the cabins were all but buried under the snow, Martha (Patty) Reed clung to her doll for comfort. CALIFORNIA DEPARTMENT OF PARKS AND RECREATION

solidly as Uncle Billy and Stanton had hoped. Despairing, Karl Burger and William Murphy, youngest of the Murphy brothers, turned back.

Twelve-year-old Lemuel struggled on, encouraged by his sisters. Impressed by his grit, a couple of the men contrived a set of snowshoes out of wayside materials. They were almost hopelessly clumsy. But the whole party was moving slowly, and the determined boy was able to hang on, up and over the pass.

Stanton was the one who caused worry. On the second day out, he dragged behind and did not reach camp until after dark.

It was the beginning of the most hideous journey in the history of the American West.

VIII

Breaking Out

An unusual sequence of sunny days crept by. For the snowshoers the good weather meant new agony. The dazzling light reflected from vast expanses of snow inflamed their eyes almost unbearably. They even welcomed the cold darkness of night. The pain in their eyes and cramped legs lessened as they sat around crackling campfires and ever so slowly ate each supper's ration—one ounce of dried beef per meal.

Eddy showed them how to build fires on platforms of green logs. Such logs burned very slowly. Fires built on them stayed out of the snow for several hours. The blazes also served as a beacon for Charles Stanton. Weak from starvation, he kept falling farther and farther behind. On the sixth night, he did not reach camp at all.

The next morning, the remaining fourteen people could see no sign of him when they peered anxiously along their back trail. When they peered ahead, their hearts sank still lower. Not a sign of human activity marked a white chaos of snow-covered meadows, steep hills, and frightening canyons. Only the tops of the trees appeared above the

Several furious storms swept across the mountains during the grim winter of 1846–47.

snow line, yet somewhere out there was a trail. But where?

They couldn't communicate with the two Indians. They suspected, moreover, that the pair didn't remember much of their crossing with Stanton. The land would have looked much different then, during summer. Only a guide who had observed landmarks very carefully could locate the way now.

But the snowshoers had no such guide. Stanton had died somewhere in the wilderness, perhaps because of their own selfishness. They had not answered his appeal for meat back at the lake.

The night before, they had eaten the last of their beef. Now they, too, realized what it meant to be totally without food. In despair, some talked of returning to the lake.

William Eddy lashed at them for their spinelessness. Dying in the camp at the lake—if they reached it—would do no one any good. Their only hope was to keep going west on their clumsy, rotting snowshoes.

He spoke out of a hidden source of strength the others knew nothing about. On one of the previous nights he had found, in an overlooked corner of his pack, about half a pound of dried bear meat. It was the piece his wife had hidden after he had killed the grizzly near the lake. She had thought it might help in a case of last resort. She had slipped it into his pack just before he had left to seek help.

Eddy must have wondered how to use the unexpected treasure. Should he share it with his thirteen companions? No! An extra ounce or so of meat probably wouldn't have saved even Stanton. But by maintaining his own strength, he increased his chances of reaching rescuers who could save his wife and children. Or so he might have thought at first. Then, apparently he grew ashamed of his selfishness. That change of mind may explain why he suddenly sought to transfer some of his strength to the others by urging them with all his power not to give up. We'll never know the truth.

We do know he took over the moral leadership of the group. That was what counted. Twenty-year-old Mary Ann Graves caught the spark he provided. Together they rallied the group, and all fourteen, twelve-year-old Lem Murphy included, wallowed on with fresh courage.

On Christmas Eve, the ninth day of their incredible

journey, a new blizzard raged down on them. With no more shelter than the lee side of a tree, they struggled to make camp. Buffeted by wind and stinging pellets of snow, some of the men hacked down green logs for a fire platform. Others dragged in dry wood. At last a blaze leaped high. Sodden, starved, and only half conscious, they crowded close to the platform for warmth.

Antonio, the young Mexican who had been hired at Independence to help care for the livestock, died unnoticed during that time of misery. Eddy realized what had happened when he saw that Antonio's hand had sagged into the fire and he was making no effort to withdraw it.

Gradually the platform and its load of fire began to sink into the snow. The green logs they had hastily hacked

The stumps show how deep the snow was at Alder Creek when the Donners' sixteen-year-old worker, Jean Baptiste Trubode, stood on top of it when helping cut down the trees for firewood. Both of the Donner brothers and probably their wives died there. CALIFORNIA DEPARTMENT OF PARKS AND RECREATION

down during the storm were too small. Heat seeped through the cracks between them to melt the snow. The semiconscious people paid no heed even when water began to rise around their feet. Then an accidental movement by one of the Indians snuffed out the flames. The coldness roused Eddy. With a supreme effort of will, he forced his companions to climb out of the well of snow. Moving like sleepwalkers, they spread out blankets and sat on them in a circle, facing inward. Eddy covered them with more blankets and then crawled in himself, closing the opening behind him. The drifting snow would cover the mound, making a kind of igloo. Warmth would come from the heat generated by their own bodies.

Engulfed by the blackness inside that mound, Patrick Dolan went raving mad. The others had to hold him down until he at last grew quiet. Along toward evening he died peacefully.

The igloo's warmth could not save Uncle Billy Graves, either. He died crowded in between his two daughters.

The storm ended the day after Christmas. Eddy pushed out of the mound and set fire to an entire dead tree. As sparks flew, the survivors gathered feebly around. But death was not yet finished. As evening approached, Lem Murphy, the youngest of the party, died with his head in the lap of one of his sisters.

Salvation lay in those corpses. They could be turned into food. Instinctively those who remained alive ignored the taboo against eating the flesh of their own kind. Instinctively, too, they realized what their hunting ancestors had learned tens of thousands of years ago. The most nourishing parts of an animal are its heart, liver, and brains. Weeping and yet fiercely joyful, they drew out their knives.

For three days they stayed in the death camp, reviving themselves. They ate part of what they had butchered and dried the rest. Each person then wrapped his or her share in a little bundle and stored it in their packs.

They were lost. They knew only that they had to keep going west no matter what cliffs or canyons stood in their way. Gradually they moved downhill, out of unbroken snow onto patches of dry ground. By then there was no meat left. They cut the webbing out of their snowshoes and tried to boil it. The gluey product didn't help. Desperate, some of the whites whispered to each other that they ought to kill the Indians for food. But murder was different from cannibalizing bodies from which life had vanished. Although Eddy was by then as hungry as the others, he warned the Indians and they slipped away.

Jay Fosdick, the husband of one of Uncle Billy's daughters, was clearly dying. The others were demoralized. Refusing to give in to the general despair, Eddy went ahead with the group's only rifle, looking for game. Mary Ann Graves went with him. After they had staggered ahead about a mile, they glimpsed a winter-thin young deer. While Mary Ann prayed, Eddy managed to lift the heavy gun and hold it steady long enough to aim and fire. The deer ran a short way and collapsed.

The bang of the gun was the last sound Fosdick heard before he died.

The bodies of the deer and of the man kept them going for a few more days. Then, by sheer chance, they came across the two Indians. Completely exhausted, the pair had dropped onto a sunny spot of dry ground to sleep. William Foster, who was delirious from hunger and suffering, took the gun from Eddy.

Eddy and three of the women—Mary Graves, her sister, Sarah Fosdick, and Amanda McCutchen—turned away. They heard two shots but did not return to share in the results. The only ones who stayed with the demented Foster were his loyal wife and her widowed sister, Harriet Murphy Pike.

For the next week, Eddy and his companions had only grass to eat. Toward the end of the period cold rains drenched them. On they stumbled down gently tilting ground until they saw footprints and followed them to an Indian village.

The startled inhabitants drew on their own small stores of acorns and acorn meal to feed them. The Fosters overtook them. By then their feet were so cut and flayed and bruised they could not walk. All but Eddy collapsed. Helped by the Indians he dragged ahead until he reached the first white habitation. It was January 17. He had been on the trail for thirty-two days.

The cabin he reached was one of several located on a place called Johnson's Ranch. The hut's occupants, the Ritchies, put him to bed. When he gasped that eight more people were stranded back in the hills, several men carrying warm clothes and packs of food went out to rescue them.

The dreadful trip was over. Of the fifteen people who had crossed Donner Pass, eight had died. All five of the women had survived.

IX

Rescue

As soon as Eddy could sit up in bed, he began planning a rescue party. It turned out to be harder than he expected. The war between the United States and Mexico had drawn most of the young Americans in California south toward Los Angeles. Those still hanging around Sutter's Fort in the Sacramento Valley were slow to embark on a project that might be more dangerous than joining the army. Moreover, they wanted guarantees that they would be paid for their work. Nearly three weeks passed before fourteen men started on horseback toward the mountains. With them they led several pack mules loaded with flour, dried beef, coffee, and warm clothing.

One of the fourteen was William Eddy. He had not yet recovered fully from his ordeal, but he was frantic with worry about his family. The least he could do, he thought, was help with the livestock.

Drenching rains beat against them. The ground became a morass of mud. Streams turned into roaring floods. On February 8, four days out of Johnson's Ranch, they reached a campground at a place called Mule Spring. Horses could

Sutter's Fort was the commercial and political heart of early California's vast Sacramento Valley. CALIFORNIA DEPARTMENT OF PARKS AND RECREATION

go no farther, for the higher slopes were piled deep with snow. The rescuers built a hut of brush and poles for storing the provisions they could not carry on their own backs. Two men were left there to guard the food from hungry animals.

Eddy and a companion drove the horses and mules back to Johnson's Ranch. There he learned to his joy that Big Bill McCutchen and Jim Reed had managed to reach California the previous fall. They had not been able to recruit help for the Donner Party, however. As mentioned earlier, most of the Americans around San Francisco Bay and in the lower Sacramento Valley had been away, fighting the

Mexican troops in southern California. Victory changed that. The triumphant volunteers began drifting back north. By holding mass meetings in the little towns around the Bay, Reed and McCutchen were finally able to raise money for supplies and sign up rescuers to go to the aid of the stranded Donners.

Meanwhile the ten men of Eddy's original rescue party were struggling single file up the canyon-seamed mountain. They leaned forward under packs weighing fifty pounds or more each. The rains had left the snow too squishy for showshoes. At each step the man in the lead sank almost to his knees in the snow. When he was worn out, he dropped to the rear of the column. The second man became the leader. Then the third and fourth and so on. That way every one shared in the killing labor of breaking out the trail.

William Eddy   *Eleanor Eddy*

The first party to force a way across the pass was kept going largely by the courage and moral stamina of William Eddy, his determination undimmed by the death of half the group along the way. But before he was well enough to return to the lake, his wife Eleanor and both their small children perished. UNIVERSITY OF UTAH LIBRARIES

As the slope grew steeper, three men dropped out. The other seven pushed on in a daze of weariness. On February 18, two weeks after leaving Johnson's, they crawled across the pass and staggered down past the frozen lake to the snow-covered cabins.

The smell and filth and vermin inside the dark huts were appalling. The people had been living on ox hides boiled in kettles until they resembled gobs of vile glue. For variety they gnawed on bones that had boiled or burned soft enough for teeth to bite into them. There was not much nourishment in either product. Four men, one woman, a fifteen-year-old boy, and two babies had died while waiting for rescue. The woman was Eddy's wife. One of the babies was also his.

The newcomers passed out part of the food they had packed. The rest they saved for the journey back to Mule Spring. They cleaned up the camp at the lake and at Alder Creek as best they could. As they worked, they realized they faced a heartbreaking dilemma. A lot of the people were too weak to cross that formidable pass. The rescue party could lead out only those who were strong enough to wade through deep snow. The weakest of the emigrants would have to stay where they were. As consolation, they would have what little food remained, and the hope that a stronger, better-equipped rescue party would soon follow the first.

Choosing those who were to go and then seeing the eyes of those who felt they were being abandoned was almost more than the rescuers could bear. Nevertheless, they picked out twenty-three people—six from Alder Creek and seventeen from the lake. There were three men, four women, and sixteen children. Some of those people were

not as strong as the rescuers hoped. One man and one child died before they were halfway to Johnson's.

At the halfway point they met Reed and McCutchen laboring upward with eight veteran mountain men. The new group had little food to spare. But, they said, a military party carrying ample supplies of provisions and clothing had been ordered to follow close behind them. It was establishing rest stops along the way. So the downhill party would soon be able to get whatever it needed.

Reed received joyful news in return. His wife, his daughter Virginia, and little Jimmy, Jr. were with the descending party. His other two children, however, were still at the lake. Anxiously he pressed on, only to be dreadfully shocked by what he found. The abandoned people at both the lake and at Alder Creek had consumed the last of their food. In desperation a few of them had turned to cannibalizing the corpses of those who had died.

James Frazier Reed was a strong, active, quick-tempered man who hoped moving to California would improve the health of his wife, Margaret. Photo believed to have been taken after the ordeal. Utah State Historical Society

After passing out the food they had, Reed and Mc-Cutchen worked out a plan on how to proceed. Like the party ahead of them, they could not take care of everyone who needed help. So they left three men behind to help those who were staying. The other seven men would help pull and push and carry the weakest of the children over the pass and down the mountain until they met the military relief party.

What follows is a sorrowful tale of bad luck, bad weather, and bad management, of betrayal, cowardice, and perhaps, murder. But there are also moments of shining heroism.

Another furious blizzard swept across the Sierra. It split

both parties into confused fragments. Virginia Reed and her little sister Patty were all but given up for dead. So was their father. Yet they rallied when they had to, as did their father. The Breens, too, almost perished. They were trapped in a great snow well created by a sinking platform. One person died there. The others survived by eating his flesh.

Much of the suffering was caused by the failure of the military party to advance beyond Mule Spring. The three men who had been left in the mountains also betrayed the trust Reed and McCutchen had placed in them. They stole valuable possessions from the people they were supposed to help. They then deserted their posts and scrambled back down the mountain loaded with loot.

The story isn't all bad, however. One example of bravery was provided by William Eddy and William Foster. They were the only two men to survive the desperate trip from the lake to Johnson's Ranch. They knew the terrors of facing Sierra weather. But when they realized the relief expeditions were in trouble, they plunged into the storm to help restore order and save lives.

Then there was Tamsen Donner, a tiny woman of great loyalty. She watched the dying of her brother-in-law, Jacob Donner, and of Jacob's wife, Elizabeth. And George Donner, Tamsen's husband, was clearly dying. The cut he had received while building their shelter on Alder Creek had become infected. He was in horrible pain and would soon have to give in to starvation.

Rescuers appeared. Tamsen could have gone out with them. George, however, would have had to stay behind, dying in his filthy bed. Tamsen said she would stay with him, keeping him as comfortable as she could, although she knew the decision would result in her own death.

A mystery surrounds the ending of her life. The puzzle revolves around Lewis Keseberg. He was thirty-two years old. At the start of the trip he had been tall and handsome. He had been well educated. But during the disintegration of the party at Donner Lake, he became crazed and wild. William Eddy and William Foster, the last rescuers to reach the death camps, hadn't strength enough to bring Keseberg out with the remaining children. They left him behind with Tamsen Donner and her dying husband. Later, some people said he killed Tamsen for her flesh. Near the end of his own life, Keseberg, poor and lonely, vigorously denied the charge. It is not likely the truth will ever be known.

Martha (Patty) Reed
CALIFORNIA DEPARTMENT OF PARKS AND RECREATION

Virginia Reed
HUNTINGTON LIBRARY

Two of the survivors of the disastrous trip from Illinois were the Reeds' daughters, Patty and Virginia. Both grew up, married, and raised families of their own. The Reeds and the Breens were the only families who did not lose at least one member during the journey.

The most commonly accepted statistic about the Donner Party says that forty-eight people survived the trip. Forty died along the trail and high in the Sierra. There was no fairness, of course, in the ways the deaths were distributed. The Reed and Breen families suffered no losses. The children of the Graves and both Donner families lost their parents. Eddy lost his entire family. Several grown-ups lost a spouse or one or more children. The heaviest death rate was among the train's bachelors.

Most of the emigrants who reached California fitted easily into the area's rapidly growing population. Those who wanted mates soon found them. Little Virginia Reed married at age fourteen. Eddy remarried and raised a new family. The Breens became civic leaders in the little town of San Juan Bautista, as did the Murphys at Marysville.

Who was primarily responsible for the tragedy? Was it Hastings, who gave bad advice but reached California with sixty-six wagons? Or did the Donners' own mistakes make the disaster inevitable? There is no easy answer.

The label "cannibals" has become firmly attached to the Donner Party. That view is too narrow. The basic story tells about a group of average Americans searching for a better life in the West. It shows how these ordinary people reacted when their dream seemed to be turning to ashes. In some ways it is a dark picture. But it is also bright with threads of courage and sharing.

Bibliography

Three authors have written full-length books about the Donner Party. The first, C. F. McGlashan, published *The History of the Donner Party* in Truckee, California in 1879. Later editions were considerably revised. McGlashan obtained much of his material from talks with survivors of the tragedy. The second major book, written by George Stewart, was *Ordeal by Hunger* (New York, 1935, reissued in 1960 with much additional material). Stewart's volume, generally considered the authority on the subject, has recently been challenged by the third author, Joseph King, *Winter of Entrapment: A New Look at the Donner Party* (Toronto, Canada, 1992). King objects primarily to what he considers Stewart's racism.

Stewart's expanded *Ordeal* contains, as supplement, three accounts by members of the ill-fated party: a diary Patrick Breen kept at the Donner Lake camp, November 20, 1846–March 1, 1847; James Reed's sparse account of his rescue trip, February 21, 1847–March 1, 1847; and the amazing letter Virginia Reed wrote about her trip to her cousin on May 16, 1847, shortly after her rescue.

Additional contemporary material is in two books by men who shared the early stages of the journey with the

Donners. One was Edwin Bryant's *What I Saw in California* (New York, 1849) and Jesse Q. Thornton's *Oregon and California in 1848* (New York, 1849). Thornton interviewed several survivors of the disaster while the events were still fresh in their minds.

James Clyman's diary of his trip east in 1846, part of it with Lansford Hastings, appears in pages 200–230 of *James Clyman, Frontiersman*, edited by Charles L. Camp (Portland, Oregon, 1960). Lansford Hastings' *The Emigrant's Guide to Oregon and California* was revived many years ago with notes by Charles Carey (Princeton, 1932).

A bare-bones diary by James Reed, covering the Donner experience from Fort Bridger to the point on the Humboldt River where Reed and Snyder battled, appears in *West of Fort Bridger . . . 1846–1850*, edited by Dale L. Morgan, Roderic Korns, Will Bagley, and Harold Schindler. (Logan, Utah, 1994).

George R. Stewart's *The California Trail* (New York, 1962) is a good overview of the entire trail. Two modern historians cast cooly appraising glances at the Donners' winter sufferings: Philip L. Fradkin, *The Seven States of California*, pages 73–80 (New York, 1995), and Arthur K. Peters, *Seven Trails West*, part of Chapter 4 (New York, 1996).

Lansford W. Hastings' career is well developed in Will Bagley, "Lansford Warren Hastings, Scoundrel or Visionary?" *Overland Journal*, Spring 1994.

The location of the two Donner Party camps during the winter of 1846–47 is established in Donald L. Hardesty, "Donner Party Archeology," *Overland Journal*, Winter, 1992.

Index

page numbers in italics refer to photo captions